DON'T WORRY, LITTLE CRAB

CHRIS HAUGHTON

"Life shrinks or expands in proportion to one's courage" Anais Nin

For Daishu, we can go anywhere :)

A huge thank you to Deirdre for her invaluable help on this book.

First published 2019 by Walker Books Ltd, 87 Vauxhall Walk, London SE11 5HJ • This edition published 2020 • © 2019 Chris Haughton • The right of Chris Haughton to be identified as author and illustrator of this work has been asserted by him in accordance with the Copyright, Designs and Patents Act 1988 • This book has been typeset in SHH Regular • Printed in Italy • All rights reserved. No part of this book may be reproduced, transmitted or stored in an information retrieval system in any form or by any means, graphic, electronic or mechanical, including photocopying, taping and recording, without prior written permission from the publisher. • British Library Cataloguing in Publication Data: a catalogue record for this book is available from the British Library • Published by arrangement with Debbie Bibo Agency • ISBN 978-1-4063-9286-9 • www.walker.co.uk • 10 9 8 7 6 5 4 3 2 1

WALKER BOOKS
AND SUBSIDIARIES
LONDON • BOSTON • SYDNEY • AUCKLAND

DON'T WORRY, LITTLE CRAB

CHRIS HAUGHTON

Little Crab and Very Big Crab
live in a tiny rockpool.

Today they're off to THE SEA!
"This is going to be so great,"
says Little Crab.

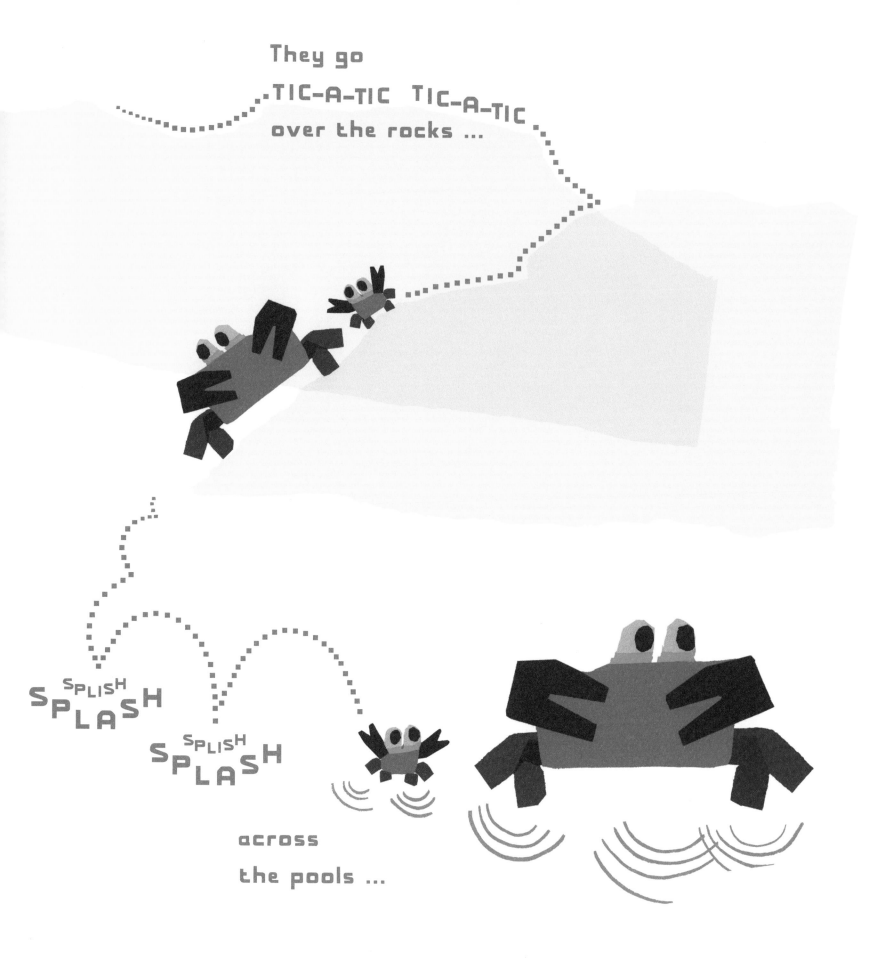

and **SQUELCH**
SQUELCH
SQUELCH

through
the
slimy
slippery
seaweed.

"I can go ANYWHERE!"
says Little Crab.

Finally they get to the very edge.
"Here we are," says Very Big Crab ...

"THE SEA!"

"Oh," says Little Crab.

"Maybe it's better
we don't go in the
sea," says Little Crab.

"Don't worry,"
says Very Big Crab.
"It will be ok."

But the waves are getting bigger...

Look! A huge wave!
Hold tight!

Here it comes!

WHOOSH!

"I think we've
had enough of
the sea now,"
says Little Crab.

"Let's just go a
little bit further,"
says Very Big Crab.
"I think you'll like it."

But the waves keep getting bigger ...
and bigger...

Another one!
Hold tight!

Here it comes!

WHOOSH!

"I don't think I like the sea,"
says Little Crab. "Maybe we
should go home."

"Don't worry, Little Crab,"
says Very Big Crab,
"I'm here. Come!
Just a few more steps..."

Little Crab
takes a
step ...

then
another ...

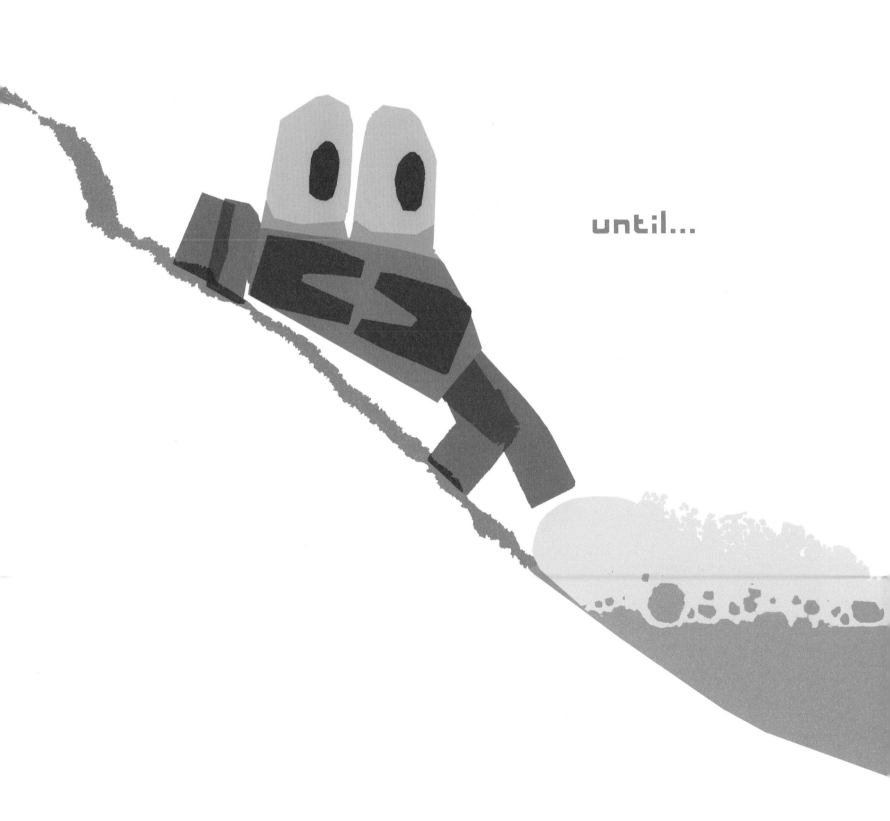

until...

"I'm in the sea!"
says Little Crab.

But then they see an **ENORMOUS** wave.

It gets bigger ...
and bigger ...
and bigger...

"Ready?" asks Very Big Crab.
Little Crab nods.

They take a deep breath.

Here it comes!

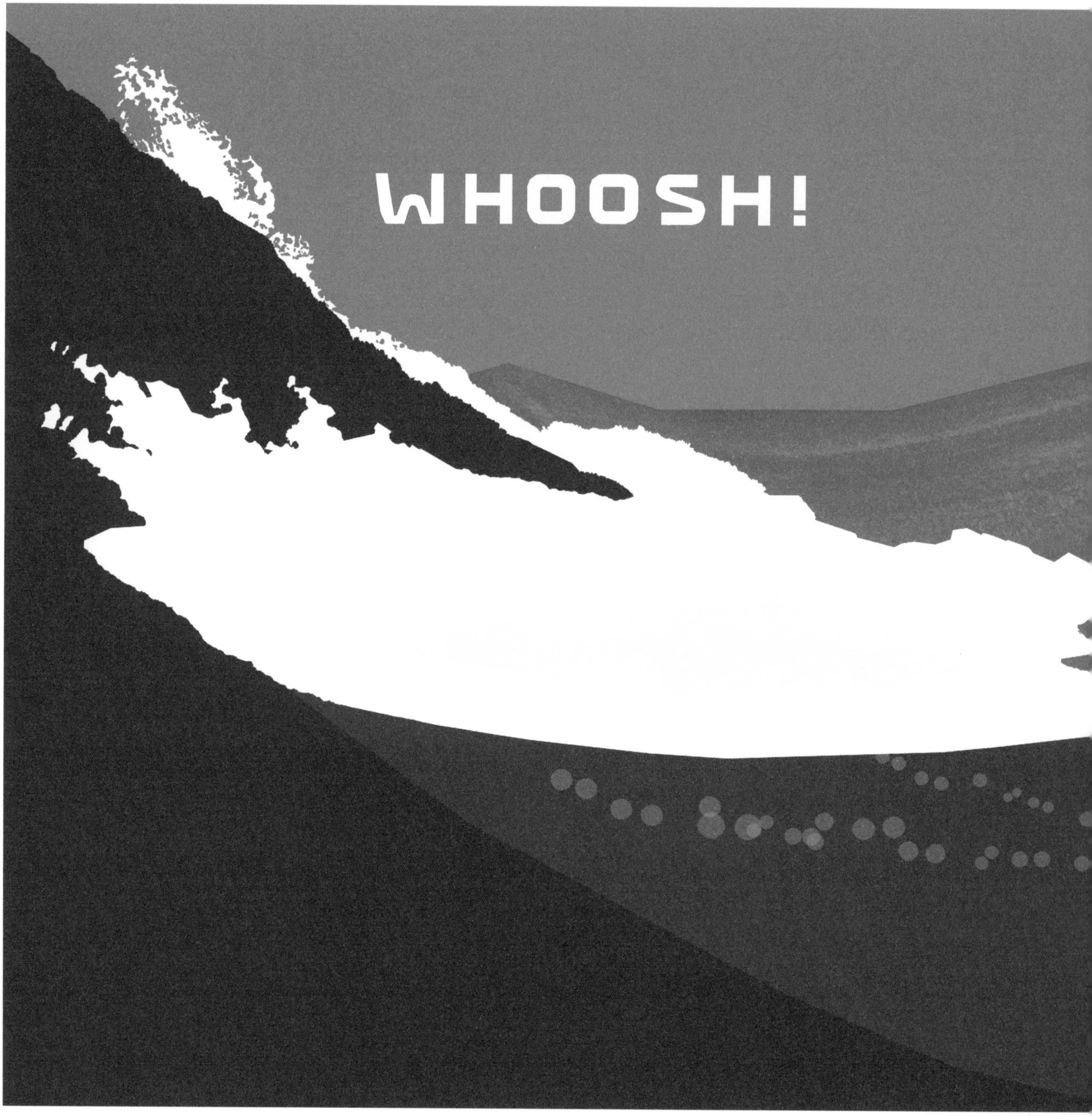
WHOOSH!

Down
down
down
they
go...

"LOOK, Little Crab!"

Everyone comes to
say hello.
"My name is Little Crab,"
says Little Crab.

They eat delicious seaweed ...

they run all across the sea floor ...

and they have a giant game of hide and seek.

"I LOVE THE SEA,"
says Little Crab.

"Yes, but it's time
to go home now,"
says Very Big Crab.

"WHAT!?
I really don't want to go home!"
says Little Crab.

"Well, how about we go
the long way home?"
says Very Big Crab.

"Can we go up this way?"
asks Little Crab.

"I think you can go anywhere,"
says Very Big Crab.
And off they went.